# Sebastian

For Sebastian, Tosca And Toppa

ISBN: 978-1-935021-27-8
Library of Congress Control Number: 2008907919

This edition first published in the United States 2009
by Mathew Price Limited,
5013 Golden Circle, Denton TX 76208
Text and illustrations copyright © 1990 Vanessa Julian-Ottie
Cover Design by Empire Design Studio
All rights reserved
Manufactured in China

Vanessa Julian-Ottie

# Sebastian

MATHEW PRICE

This is Sebastian, always the odd one out, heading for the cat flap.

Outside, Sebastian sniffed new smells and heard new sounds.

"What was that? Who's there?" A little face peeped though a hole in the rocks.

"Ow! Ow! Ow!" cried Sebastian.
"That hurt!"

Sebastian limped towards the fence.
"What sort of animal is that?" he said.

"Hello," said the go
said the ducks. Bu
said a word. He fe

Beyond the duck pond was a drainpipe.
Sebastian looked and looked.
Was that a mouse at the other end?
He pounced.

*Kersplosh!* Where did that mouse go?

Sebastian found a mouse in the barn. He didn't know somebody was watching him.

"Help!"
He'd never seen a horse before.
He won't hurt you, Sebastian.
But watch out behind you!

Sebastian ran for the gap in the old
stone wall as fast as his legs could go.

Sebastian squeezed through just in time.
He headed straight for home. He never
saw the rabbits who had been playing
hide-and-seek in the garden all day.

He didn't stop running until he got
to his own front door.

Mother Cat was glad to see him back,
and he was just in time for dinner.

Sebastian Explores

Vanessa Julian-Ottie

Also in this series:
*Sebastian Explores*